D1560167

DINOSAUR

DO'S & DON'T'S

by Syd Hoff

Windmill Books and E. P. Dutton
New York

Text Copyright © 1975 by Syd Hoff and Robert Kraus
Illustrations copyright © 1975 by Syd Hoff

Published by Windmill Books & E. P. Dutton & Co.
201 Park Avenue South, New York, New York 10003

LIBRARY OF CONGRESS CATALOGING IN PUBLICATION DATA

Hoff, Sydney. Dinosaur do's & don't's.

SUMMARY: Dinosaur demonstrates proper etiquette,
health practices, and general conduct.

1. Children—Conduct of life. [1. Etiquette.
2. Conduct of life] I. Kraus, Robert,
joint author. II. Title.
BJ1631.H55 1975 170'.202'22 75-6509 ISBN 0-525-61530-X

Published simultaneously in Canada by Clarke,
Irwin & Company, Limited, Toronto and Vancouver

Printed in the U.S.A.
10 9 8 7 6 5 4 3 2

DINOSAURS DO

get out of bed when their
mothers call.

DINOSAURS DON'T

skate in the house.

DINOSAURS DO

take baths without being told.

DINOSAURS DON'T

**ask their mothers to buy them
everything they see.**

DINOSAURS DO

ask permission before they go
out to play.

DINOSAURS DON'T

interrupt when people
are talking.

DINOSAURS DO

wear their boots when
it's slushy.

DINOSAURS DON'T

gobble their food.

DINOSAURS DO

**write letters to grandparents
who live far away.**

DINOSAURS DON'T

play with matches.

DINOSAURS DO

take care of library books.

DINOSAURS DON'T

read other people's mail.

DINOSAURS DO

say, "Thank you."

DINOSAURS DON'T

eat between meals.

DINOSAURS DO

wear their glasses.

DINOSAURS DON'T

throw their baseball bats.

DINOSAURS DO

practice their piano lessons.

DINOSAURS DON'T

grab.

DINOSAURS DO

stay indoors when it rains.

DINOSAURS DON'T

play favorites.

DINOSAURS DO

return borrowed things.

DINOSAURS DON'T

gossip.

DINOSAURS DO

keep quiet while people are
on the phone.

DINOSAURS DON'T

push others around.

DINOSAURS DO

cover up when they sneeze.

DINOSAURS DON'T

cheat.

DINOSAURS DO

**brush their teeth after
every meal.**

DINOSAURS DON'T

mistreat animals.

DINOSAURS DO

remove their hats in the house.

DINOSAURS DON'T

give excuses when they lose.

DINOSAURS DO

apologize when they're wrong.

DINOSAURS DON'T

cross against the light.

DINOSAURS DO

flush the toilet.

DINOSAURS DON'T

litter.

DINOSAURS DO

wipe their feet.

DINOSAURS DON'T

slouch.

DINOSAURS DO

help senior citizens.

DINOSAURS DON'T

play their TVs too loud.

DINOSAURS DON'T

leave their toys all over the house.

DINOSAURS DO

**know their addresses in case
they get lost.**

DINOSAURS DON'T

wait until the last minute to
do their homework.

DINOSAURS DO

take their medicine.

DINOSAURS DON'T

leave the refrigerator open.

DINOSAURS DO

say, "Excuse me."

DINOSAURS DON'T

stay up past their bedtime.